THE KID'S USER GUIDE TO A
HUMAN LIFE
BOOK TWO: AN OPEN HEART

THE KID'S USER GUIDE TO A

HUMAN LIFE

BOOK TWO: AN OPEN HEART

REBECCA BRENNER

NEW YORK

THE KID'S USER GUIDE TO A **HUMAN LIFE**
BOOK TWO: AN OPEN HEART

© 2016 **REBECCA BRENNER**. Illustrated by **BROOKE KEMMERER**.

Published in New York, New York, by Morgan James Publishing. Morgan James and The Entrepreneurial Publisher are trademarks of Morgan James, LLC.
www.MorganJamesPublishing.com

The Morgan James Speakers Group can bring authors to your live event. For more information or to book an event visit The Morgan James Speakers Group at www.TheMorganJamesSpeakersGroup.com.

Shelfie

A **free** eBook edition is available with the purchase of this print book.

CLEARLY PRINT YOUR NAME ABOVE IN UPPER CASE

Instructions to claim your free eBook edition:
1. Download the Shelfie app for Android or iOS
2. Write your name in **UPPER CASE** above
3. Use the Shelfie app to submit a photo
4. Download your eBook to any device

ISBN 978-1-63047-866-7 paperback
ISBN 978-1-63047-867-4 eBook
ISBN 978-1-63047-868-1 hardcover
Library of Congress Control Number:
2015919849

Cover Design by:
Chris Treccani
www.3dogdesign.net

Interior Design by:
Bonnie Bushman
bonnie@caboodlegraphics.com

In an effort to support local communities and raise awareness and funds, Morgan James Publishing donates a percentage of all book sales for the life of each book to Habitat for Humanity Peninsula and Greater Williamsburg

Get involved today, visit
www.MorganJamesBuilds.com

Habitat
for Humanity®
Peninsula and
Greater Williamsburg
Building Partner

For Papi – Thank you for sharing
your Open Heart with me
—RB

For Jacob – for showing me
how to reside in my Heart
—BK

INTRODUCTION

"You must live in the present, launch yourself on every wave, find your eternity in each moment. Fools stand on their island of opportunities and look toward another land. There is no other land; there is no other life but this."

—Henry David Thoreau

O n our last adventure in *The Kid's User Guide to a Human Life, Book One: An Open Mind,* you began the journey of looking deeply into your own self. You started by exploring the structure of your brain, your Inner Navigator. You saw how your brain is hardwired by billions of neurons and the pathways they create throughout your brain called neuron pathways. Even though all brains have essentially the same parts, how yours is wired is unique to you!

You looked at how your brain takes in information from all around you to inform the neurons on which pathways to create. You learned how your family interactions and dynamics, the community you live in, your friendships, your education, the music you listen to, the books you read and the television shows you watch all create pathways in your brain. It was quite an awesome discovery to learn that all the information you take in from the world around you and how you process it creates your neuron pathways, which in many ways make you You!

You saw how this You comes alive through what you are saying to yourself all day—your own Chattering Mind. You looked deeply into how your Chattering Mind is a noisy place— repetitive, habitual and many times negative. You noticed how the Chattering Mind, when left unchecked, moves you into an automatic and unconscious way of being.

You glimpsed how this automatic way of being keeps your chatter focused on a small set of experiences, looping continuously and filtering everything you do through this repetitive loop. You began to see how this limits the natural openness of your true adventurous self. And how this in turn limits your experience of the magic of your life unfolding moment by moment.

You explored how your Chattering Mind influences your nervous system—an amazing and intricate communication network between your body, emotions and mind. You learned about the parasympathetic nervous system, which is a resting, health-enhancing mode of the nervous system that gets turned on when it registers feelings of contentment and safety. You also learned about the sympathetic nervous system, which is an alarm mode of the nervous system that activates when you feel fear, anger or worry. Most importantly, you saw how most times, the sympathetic

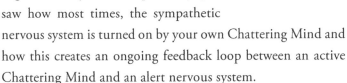

nervous system is turned on by your own Chattering Mind and how this creates an ongoing feedback loop between an active Chattering Mind and an alert nervous system.

You also explored your own Open Mind. You discovered how your Open Mind's home is in the Present Moment and that when you bring your Inner Attention into the Present Moment you can connect to your Open Mind. This connection allows you to feel more present, peaceful and alive. You discovered how this connection to your Open Mind gives you a direct relationship with your own adventurous life as it is unfolding. And you began to see clearly how your ability to know and live from your Open Mind and consciously use your Chattering Mind as a tool assists you more than anyone or anything else on your journey through life. This was an exciting discovery because it gave you a choice—to either go along unconsciously with the old habits of your Chattering Mind or to begin to place your Inner Attention in the spaciousness of your Open Mind.

Lastly, you discovered three tools which you carry with you always to bring you Inner Attention back to the present moment and into your Open Mind—Breath Awareness, Body Awareness and Awareness of the Silence. Each time your Inner Attention wanders into the automatic way of being through the Chattering Mind, and you notice that, you now know you can use the sensations of your Breath, Body and Quiet to connect you back to the fullness of your own Open Mind and the aliveness of the Present Moment.

The beginnings of your adventure in *Book One: An Open Mind* revealed to you that when you are present you are connected to the qualities of the moment, like openness and aliveness. When you are present, you can see clearly what is happening before you and make the most intelligent choice in that moment. When you are present,

you are connected to deep courage, bravery and patience—giving you the ability to open to all of the joy, sorrow and challenge this human life will surely bring. You saw how when your Inner Attention is placed consciously and wisely in your Open Mind you are able to bravely live this adventurous life to its fullest!

In *Book Two: An Open Heart* your adventure of looking deeply into your self and this human life continues. During this part of your journey, you'll look at how Life isn't very solid, but more like a river. Thoughts, experiences and emotions constantly flow in and out of your Open Mind and Awareness. You'll explore how your Chattering Mind unconsciously interacts with this boundless and groundless flow. And you'll look at how when the mysterious flow of life is met bravely and consciously from your Open Mind it begins to connect you back to the qualities of your own Open Heart, your true home.

CHAPTER 1

"Knowing others is wisdom, knowing yourself is enlightenment."

—Lao Tzu

When you are living only from your Chattering Mind you see yourself as a solid, set self. Your Chattering Mind has an entire story of who you think you are—a son, a daughter, a student, a soccer player, a good kid or a bad kid. Your Chattering Mind has created an entire solid-feeling persona based on these roles. It feels so solid that when you first meet someone, after telling them your name, you quickly follow with telling them all the roles you play. The habit of thinking of yourself in this way is so strong that at first it feels strange to even question it.

However, everything about you is continually shifting and changing. Look more closely at what you normally take to be the solid you—your body, Chattering Mind, emotions, perceptions and experiences. Pay attention long enough and you'll begin to see that these parts of you are all in a constant state of flux. You are more like a living river of changing sensations, experiences, feelings and thoughts. The reality is that nothing about you or life is static. So let's begin this adventure by asking, "Who am I really?"

Let's go back to your persona—built on the roles you play. Maybe you first answer the question "Who am I really?" with the answer "These roles"—a daughter, a son, a sister, a brother. seem really solid at first vever, the roles you play your life are always

changing. Sometimes the student, sometimes the teacher, for part of your life the child, maybe someday the parent. One year the artist, the next a musician. Sometimes the good student, sometimes the struggling student. As you move through your adventure, you'll play many different roles. Sometimes, even multiple roles in one day.

So maybe you go on to answer "Who am I really?" by saying you are your body, your physical form. But if you look closely, you'll see your physical body is definitely not static. You are roughly one centimeter taller in the morning than you are by the end of each day. You shed about 600,000 particles of skin every hour. Each day you lose about 60,100 strands of hair. You get a new stomach lining every three to four days. Your nose and ears never stop growing. And your body produces 300 billion new cells every day! Once you had the body of an infant, then a toddler, now an adolescent and eventually an adult. Your body is not some solid, fixed entity. It is a living system in constant flux.

Begin to pay attention to your senses. They are bringing in a continuous changing stream of sensations and experiences. What your eyes see is never really the same—shifting light and shadows, changing colors and hues. Your nose brings in an always-changing smellscape from the moment you awaken—smells from your breakfast, the shower, the breeze on your way to school.

Sounds are always fluctuating as they enter your ears—loud, soft, high and low. Tastes are continually arriving and disappearing from your tongue—sweet, sour, spicy, bland. Your skin is constantly bringing in sensations from your environment—clothes, weather and the embrace from a loved one. A river of experience and sensation is continually pouring through you and your senses.

So then you might answer, "I am my thoughts, my Chattering Mind." But look and you'll see that your mind and thoughts work much the same way. If you look closely and openly at your Chattering Mind you'll see that your thoughts arise naturally then dissolve on their own. One moment you may think an idea you have is great and the next moment you may think it's foolish. Even the stickiest thoughts, when allowed time and space, eventually shift, change or transform. A thought that may have caused your Chattering Mind great distress a year ago is now a faint memory.

Emotions follow this same dynamic pattern. When allowed their natural flow, they tend to surge up like a wave then pass on their own. You may wake up one morning feeling down. By lunch you may feel overjoyed spending time with your friends. By the end of lunch you may feel annoyed by these same friends. And then that night at home you may feel lonely for your friends.

You see, the "you" your Chattering Mind takes to be so solid is actually always shifting and changing—year to year, month to month, week to week, day to day, moment to moment and even second to second. No part of you is ever the same. So then, who are you really?

KEEP IT SIMPLE, ADVENTUROUS ONE

Your breath is always in the present moment. Every time you place your Inner Attention on your breath, you step out of the small, solid-feeling Chattering Mind and back into the flow of life.

Breath Awareness

Wherever you are, when you "wake up" to the fact that you are not present and lost in your Chattering Mind, kindly invite your Inner Attention to your breath.

Follow the experience of your breath with your Inner Attention. Really *feel* what it feels like to breathe—the tickle of air through your nose, the expanding of your ribs fully, the feeling of release as you exhale.

As you feel your breath, stay connected to the spaciousness of your Open Mind. Let the spaciousness of your Open Mind into your attention. Feel your aliveness. Remember, you are not just your Chattering Mind.

CHAPTER 2

"Seek not that the things which happen should happen as you wish; but wish the things which happen to be as they are, and you will have a tranquil flow of life."

—Epictetus

his dynamic life is constantly flowing through you. Life pours in through your senses creating different sensations, experiences, thoughts and emotions. Yet how is it that your Chattering Mind feels so solid if every part of you is always in flux?

Your Chattering Mind naturally registers the flow of life as it comes in as *Like, Dislike* or *Indifference.* Your Chattering Mind then begins to build a solid sense of self by Attaching to what you *Like*, Resisting what you *Dislike* and Checking Out when you are *Indifferent.* This constant, unconscious categorizing begins to cut you off from the dynamic, alive Present Moment Adventurer you truly are. Most of the time this process happens so fast and unconsciously that you are unaware that you are labeling your experiences and yourself this way. So let's look a bit closer…

When you *Like* something, your Chattering Mind Attaches to it, even grasping after it and clinging. Imagine eating ice cream on a hot summer day with a friend. The sensation of the cold dessert is refreshing. The taste of the sugar and cream is satisfying. And the experience of sharing with your friend is uplifting. You start to see yourself as someone who likes ice cream.

On the surface, this doesn't seem like a big deal. But what happens when your love for certain ice cream flavors changes? Or you come to dislike eating ice cream on cold days? You may even start to prefer smoothies instead of ice cream. Or what if you become allergic to ice cream altogether?

When you *Like* an experience, your Chattering Mind builds an entire story around how much this experience reflects who you are. Over time, you keep telling yourself that story and you take it to be solid and undeniably true. When you are able to repeat the experience you are happy. But when you can't, you are unhappy and defeated. Your Chattering Mind may even go as far as to declare that you could never be happy unless you have it.

The same is true for experiences that you *Dislike*. When you don't like something, your Chattering Mind Resists it. Imagine you are caught in a rainstorm without an umbrella or raincoat. You are wearing your favorite outfit and you're getting drenched! This is not what you wanted to happen today, yet here you are soaking wet. For most Adventurers, an inner Resistance quickly comes up—"I don't like this! Why is this happening to me? I don't want this to happen to me!"

When you *Dislike* an experience your Chattering Mind pushes it away— sometimes internally, sometimes physically and sometimes both. And your Resistance surely worsens the situation. You are getting wet and it feels cold and miserable, yes. However, adding anger and Resistance to this situation will only increase your distress.

Your Chattering Mind also builds an entire set story about your Resistance being who you are—"Nothing ever goes my way! Why do bad things always happen to me?" And getting caught in this only narrows your Chattering Mind's perception and small sense of self.

At other times, you are *Indifferent* to your experiences. Things you do over and over every single day tend to register as benign. During activities like brushing your teeth and hair, eating the same old breakfast and getting dressed and off to school you Check Out. If you begin to pay attention, you'll notice that as you move through these activities, you're not at all present. Most times, you'll find your Inner Attention lost unconsciously in the noise of the Chattering Mind.

When you are *Indifferent* to an experience, you move into an automatic way of being. Without paying attention or being very present, you automatically move through your day in Chattering Mind mode. You may be brushing your teeth physically, but mentally you are going through a conversation or experience with your best friend. This seems harmless enough, but when you look closely you'll see this makes you out of touch with and forgetful of the alive, dynamic quality of life. And this may be happening the majority of your days! This continually keeps you out of touch with the alive, dynamic Adventurer you truly are.

Attachment, Resistance and Checking Out happen countless times each day. However, when your Chattering Mind is unconsciously Attaching to the experiences you *Like*,

Resisting the experiences you *Dislike*, and Checking Out during the experiences that cause *Indifference,* you are unknowingly solidifying a small, solid-feeling sense of self. Lost in your small self, you begin to forget the awake, aware and dynamic Adventurer you really are.

Like, Dislike and *Indifference* are also the starting point for all of your emotions. When you consciously allow emotions to flow through your own Awake Awareness and Open Mind, they bring clarity and connect you deeply to your life as it unfolds moment to moment. When you are unconsciously lost in emotions, they tend to reinforce the small sense of the Chattering Mind. And being lost in the small self is uncomfortable at best and painful at worst. Seeing this more clearly will give you a greater understanding of your emotions, allowing you to have a brave and courageous relationship with them. And beginning to have a brave and courageous relationship with your emotions will lead you closer to answering, "Who am I really?"

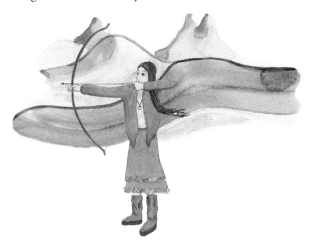

KEEP IT SIMPLE, ADVENTUROUS ONE

The sensations of your body are also always unfolding in the present moment. Your beating heart, the feeling of your feet in your shoes on the ground, the texture of your clothes on your skin are all bridges to bring your Inner Attention out of your Chattering Mind and back into the present moment.

Body Awareness

When you "wake up" to the fact that your Inner Attention is lost in your Chattering Mind, kindly invite your Inner Attention to the *feeling* of your whole body.

Feel your feet in your shoes placed firmly on the ground. Feel the wind and sun on your skin. Feel the sensation of your palms resting on your legs.

As you experience the feeling of your body, stay grounded in the openness of your Open Mind. Bravely live into, with your Inner Attention, the spaciousness of your Open Mind.

CHAPTER 3

"Emotion arises at the place where mind and body meet. It is the body's reaction to your mind—or you might say, a reflection of your mind in the body."

—Eckhart Tolle

When you *Like* something—a thought, a person or an experience—and you are functioning from your Chattering Mind, you Attach or cling to that experience. Imagine your favorite outfit. You love how it fits, looks and feels. You wear that outfit at least once a week. It feels like a true reflection of your style and personality.

Now imagine that your younger sister has asked to borrow this outfit on the same day you plan to wear it. She has a big presentation in science class and wants to look her best. Reacting from your Chattering Mind, you quickly and aggressively say, "No Way! That is MY outfit!" As your sister leaves your room defeated, you think, "How could she even think for a minute I'd give up my favorite outfit? I need this outfit!"

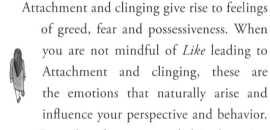

Attachment and clinging give rise to feelings of greed, fear and possessiveness. When you are not mindful of *Like* leading to Attachment and clinging, these are the emotions that naturally arise and influence your perspective and behavior. Even though you succeeded in thwarting your sister's attempt to borrow your clothes, you are left with these feelings swimming through you. And no Adventurer ever feels at home when greed and fear lurk within.

Emotions and thoughts such as greed and fear also change the chemistry of your body by turning on the stress response. When the stress response is activated, your brain quickly sends signals down your spinal cord, through your nerves and to your adrenal glands telling them to release the hormone adrenaline. When released, adrenaline increases the amount of sugar in your blood, increases your heart rate and raises your blood pressure.

Your brain's remarkable hypothalamus simultaneously signals your pituitary gland to stimulate your adrenal cortex into producing a stress hormone called cortisol. Cortisol keeps your blood sugar and blood pressure elevated to give you energy to escape from danger.

So here you are—your actions, thoughts and subsequent emotions over your sister's desire to wear your outfit have now created an entire biochemical response in your body. Stress hormones, high blood sugar and rising blood pressure now have to run their course. Unfortunately, this is physically, mentally and emotionally uncomfortable. And many times your Chattering Mind's grasping creates an ongoing loop with the physical responses in your body. They begin to feed one another, looping continuously, and can lead to anxiety, obsessive thinking or depression.

However, when what you *Like* is met from your present Open Mind the feelings that naturally follow are joy, kindness and generosity. Imagine being present and open when your sister explains that your favorite outfit would help her breeze through her presentation with confidence and ease. Chances are you would feel the grasping of wanting to hold on to your outfit, but at the same time recognize that you would enjoy helping out your sister.

You remember how nervous you get when you have to present in class and you would like to ease that discomfort for your little sister. You've got plenty of other great clothes anyway or maybe an even better outfit to share. Because of staying connected to your Open Mind you are able to bravely be with your own Attachment and clinging and then step beyond it and open to the truly kind Adventurer you are.

This conscious "stepping beyond" also creates a chemical change in your body. As you bring your Inner Attention to your Open Mind and deepen your breath, you are able to move your diaphragm fully, thereby activating the vagus nerve, which in turn activates your parasympathetic nervous system. From here your heart rate slows down creating a deeper sense of ease, blood vessels dilate oxygenating your blood and lungs, digestion is activated releasing nutrients into your body and energy is restored.

At the same time, your prefrontal cortex becomes accessible. Your prefrontal cortex, when activated, suppresses negative emotions, quiets the reactionary part of the brain called the amygdala and increases your ability to think clearly. You may decide to not share your outfit, but chances are you will be open and kind, creating space for you and your sister to find a resolution.

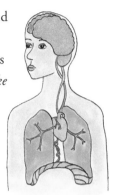

Emotions and the physical changes they create come when you *Dislike* something as well. Normally, when you *Dislike* something and you are functioning unconsciously from your small, habitual Chattering Mind, the tendency is to Resist. Imagine summer has just begun and you take a fall on your bike and break your arm. You experience immense pain from the break and great discomfort from the cast. And now you learn that having a cast means you can't go swimming for six to eight weeks! You are simultaneously fuming and devastated. You do not want this to be your summer! You spend your days lost in your own mental anguish over your ruined summer.

This Resistance gives rise to feelings such as fear, anger, depression and anxiety. When you're not mindful of *Dislike* leading to Resistance, these emotions arise and influence how you see yourself, your situation and the world. The stress response is signaled to kick on, leaving you with the pain of your initial hurt and your painful Resistance and now your nervous system is working from a heightened state. Not only have you broken your arm, but now you are so upset that you can't find any pleasure in anything. The summer looks like a long empty expanse ahead.

However, when *Dislike* moves through you and you open bravely to it, instead of closing down around Resistance, emotions such as acceptance, clarity and compassion begin to arise. You're bummed about your broken arm, and from your own Open Mind you are able to meet that disappointment with compassion. Your own compassion grows towards all the other kids who are hurt or sick just like you this summer. You are also able to see that although being hurt is not ideal, there is still a lot of fun and adventure to be had. Your awareness of how *Dislike* brings Resistance helps to support the activation of your parasympathetic nervous system and prefrontal cortex. And this mentally and physically sets you up to courageously step beyond your Resistance and accept the reality of your situation.

When you are *Indifferent* to Life as it moves through you, you tend to Check Out and disconnect from the moment, living mainly in your Chattering Mind. If you pay attention the next time you are doing your chores, you will notice this tendency. Most times, while cleaning your room or taking out the garbage, you are just trying to get it done so you can get onto the next thing. This moving mindlessly through your moments gives rise to feelings of boredom, spaciness and non-presence.

When you bring your Open Mind to the activities you are *Indifferent* to, you brighten your own presence and awaken feelings such as peace, contentment and aliveness. When you take the garbage out you can closely pay attention to the graceful movement of your feet as they move, the cool night air on you skin and the mystery of the stars in the sky above. As you consciously take in these moments, notice the feelings of peace, gratitude and contentment that surely follow.

Consciously, from your Open Mind, noticing the moments of *Like, Dislike* and *Indifference* creates a space to clearly see how your Attachment and Resistance create your emotions and how, when lost in the Chattering Mind, this leads to feeling like a small, solid self. In understanding how your emotions begin and flow, you can use your Open Mind to have a conscious relationship with them and remember the dynamic, open Adventurer you are.

With clear seeing, you can bravely open to all of life—the good, the bad and the benign. This brave opening creates a space for the qualities of your Open Heart to awaken. From your Open Mind and Open Heart, you can respond consciously and directly to the flow of life, bringing freshness to each experience and a deeper knowing of who you truly are.

KEEP IT SIMPLE, ADVENTUROUS ONE

Your Chattering Mind is a loud and active place most days. And the more your Chattering Mind is stimulated by television, computers, smart phones, video games and music, the louder and more solid-feeling your Chattering Mind becomes. Underneath all the noise of our technological world and the Chattering Mind is a ground of silence. You can hear it when you switch off all your electronic devices and allow your Inner Attention to step out of your inner dialogue and into the spacious clarity of the quiet.

Awareness of Silence

When you notice your Inner Attention is lost in the fog of your Chattering Mind, kindly invite your Inner Attention out of your chatter and into the silence around you.

If you need to unplug everything, go for it! You may even need to get outside to a quiet spot under a tree.

As you shift your Inner Attention to silence, allow the spaciousness of the silence into your Inner Attention. Let the space of the quiet remind you of the space of your Open Mind. Bravely live into the spaciousness of your Open Mind by consciously and continuously hearing the space of the silence.

CHAPTER 4

"We shall not cease from exploration, and the end of all our exploring will be to arrive where we started and know the place for the first time."

—T.S. Eliot

pening bravely to the flow of life, to your *Likes* and *Dislikes*, Attachments and Resistance and all of the emotions that follow naturally moves you out of the small, solid-feeling Chattering Mind and closer to who you really are. You are not just your always-changing Chattering Mind. You are not just your ever-shifting *Likes* and *Dislikes*. You are more than your fluctuating Attachments and Resistance. And you are surely not your always-passing emotions.

Bravely opening to the flow of life and to your thoughts, feelings and emotions creates a natural space. And resting your Inner Attention in this space allows room for the fundamental qualities of your Open Heart—compassion, kindness, joy and acceptance—to awaken. There is nothing magical, mystical or romantic about the qualities of your Open Heart. Compassion, kindness, joy and acceptance are fundamental to being human. However, they easily get lost under all the noise in your Chattering Mind. Through practice you are able to cultivate them when you consciously let the stories go and bravely open to the flow of life.

Opening fully to the flow of life naturally awakens your compassion. Think back to the example of breaking your arm. When you were unconsciously caught up in *Dislike* and Resistance to your broken arm, this led to feelings of fear, anger and anxiety. However, when you were able

to courageously open to your situation and discomfort, you created the space for your natural compassion to arise towards yourself and others in your situation.

You noticed you were lost and disconnected from the aliveness of you in the present moment. You could see and feel how this felt small, confining and even painful. And you remembered to come out of your Chattering Mind and into your Open Mind, compassionately and bravely being with your Chattering Mind's stories and emotions.

This led you to know first-hand how easy it is to get lost and disconnected from the moment. You now know how uncomfortable it is to feel like a small, static, stuck self. So when you see family members, friends or even strangers lost in their Chattering Mind's stories about a challenging situation, you understand where they really  are. This understanding naturally awakens your desire to help and support—your compassion.

Opening bravely to the flow of life wakes up your natural kindness. Remember the example of sharing your favorite outfit with your sister? When you met *Like* with your Open Mind, you were able to open to your kindness and generosity. You may not have shared your favorite outfit, but in your kindness you were able to help support your sister. You see how deeply connected we are to one another. Not only do we share the same air, water and planet with every being, but the life that flows through you flows through every life form on the planet. Shaking off your own small Chattering Mind and seeing the largeness of your interconnectedness reveals that being kind to everyone you meet is the only thing that really makes sense.

This kindness spills over into how you see the stories of your own Chattering Mind. The worry, the judgment, the fear all come from the Chattering Mind's sense of being small and disconnected. You are kinder to yourself when you recognize you are lost in your Attachment and Resistance. You remember this small self isn't the whole story. Remembering and feeling your connectedness with all of life creates a space for kindness towards your own limiting stories for what they are— just stories.

When you are courageously opening to the flow of life, you are naturally more joyful. Think back to the example of the tendency to Check Out during your chores and how this dulls your experience of life. When you wake up your senses to the warmth of the dishwater on your hands or the largeness of the night sky as you take the garbage out, a natural joy and aliveness awakens in you. You are intimately connected to the cosmos, the earth and this intelligent life flowing through everyone.

Opening to this connection allows you to relax and go more confidently with the flow. Joyfully, you understand that you are so much more than your small, repetitive Chattering Mind. You see clearly the intelligent and interconnected flow of life that moves the planets and stars, shifts winter into spring and flawlessly moves you from being a baby to a toddler to a teen. From your Open Mind you can acknowledge and joyfully feel the mystery and the goodness of your human life unfolding moment by moment.

And in going with the flow, you naturally awaken your acceptance and wise responsiveness. With an Open Mind, you can begin to accept what the flow of life brings your way week to week, day to day and moment to moment. You know from experience that when things are going terribly wrong, when your day is a mess from the very beginning, you aren't failing in some way.

Life is sometimes like this. Sometimes good experiences, sometimes bad. Sometimes happy, sometimes sad. Sometimes peace, sometimes frustration. From your Open Mind and Open Heart, you can bravely accept what is here today and begin to respond wisely instead of unconsciously reacting from your Chattering Mind.

As you use your Open Mind to bravely open to the flow of life, you will deeply begin to trust your ability to experience and feel ALL this adventurous life has to offer. This human life asks

this of each Adventurer—to feel and experience it all. You, brave Adventurer, must open wisely to your Chattering Mind, feelings and emotions. It is only through fully opening that you can really experience and know how powerful, brave and wise you are. And this may be the biggest adventure of your human life—to wake up your Open Mind and know your Open Heart as home.

CHAPTER 5

"Being peacefully in relationship to everything made me realize that my happiness isn't based on the situation being "this way" or "that way"—my happiness is one which embraces my sadness, and my love is one which embraces my own hate."

—Ram Dass

Daily Practices

Like and *Dislike* and Attachment and Resistance come to every Adventurer continuously, and emotions naturally follow. This is a sure part of life. You can, through practice, have a conscious relationship with this process. Instead of getting stuck in the small habits of your Chattering Mind and the energy of your emotions, you can mindfully use them to awaken your own Open Mind and Open Heart.

Practicing with *Like, Dislike*, and *Indifference*

It can be very challenging at first to open to your feelings and emotions as they are happening. The habit of getting swept into the Chattering Mind's story and physical sensations is strong in all Adventurers. So, a good place to start is to pay attention to where emotions begin—the feelings of *Like, Dislike* and *Indifference*.

Consciously beginning to see clearly and name *Like, Dislike* and *Indifference* when they arise and the emotions that naturally follow will help you to step out of the Chattering Mind's closed system of reactions and suspend the stress response. This creates some space around your feelings and emotions. And this space begins to bring you back to your Open Mind and remind you of the fluid, dynamic Adventurer you truly are.

Keep It Simple: Seeing your *Likes*, *Dislikes* and *Indifference*

- As you move through your day, notice and name when you *Like, Dislike* or are *Indifferent* to an object, situation, experience or person.
- Seeing and naming your *Likes, Dislikes* and *Indifference* begins to return your awareness to your Open Mind and the Present Moment, moving out of the closed system of the Chattering Mind.
- Consciously note the strong pull to get caught up in what follows *Like, Dislike* and *Indifference*— Attachment and Resistance. At the same time notice how noticing brings you into a conscious relationship with your experience!
- Allow this conscious relationship to move you back into your Open Mind and Open Heart.
- Let your Breath Awareness, Body Awareness and Awareness of Silence be anchors for you in the Present Moment.

Practicing with Attachment and Resistance

Seeing your Chattering Mind—how it Attaches continually to pleasure and Resists what it considers challenging—takes a lot of courage. Sometimes monumental courage. Because what you are really doing is opening bravely and fully to this always flowing, shifting, mysterious and oftentimes difficult life. And in doing this, you must bravely open to what follows *Like, Dislike* and *Indifference*—all of your Attachment and Resistance and the emotions and sensations that follow.

This means, Brave Adventurer, that you must fully open to what you consider pleasant, as well as unpleasant, without getting lost in either.

Keep It Simple: Feeling Attachment and Resistance

- When you notice that your Chattering Mind is Attaching or Resisting, name the feeling, drop your Inner Attention out of the Chattering Mind's story and open fully to the feelings in your body.

- Opening fully simply means, as much as you are able to in the moment, from your Inner Attention *feel* the *experience* of Attachment or Resistance in your body without getting swept into your Chattering Mind's story about it.

- Use your Breath Awareness, Body Awareness and Awareness of Silence as anchors for your Inner Attention.

- Anchoring your Inner Attention in this way will help you stay out of the story and in the Present Moment.

- Pay attention to how the sensations of Attachment and Resistance arise and eventually pass through you. What is left? With practice, you'll notice you were able to bravely open, without unconsciously getting swept out of your Open Mind and Open Heart!

Practicing with a Strong Emotion

Once *Like, Dislike* or *Indifference* has turned into Attachment, Resistance or Indifference, strong emotions naturally follow. As you saw in the previous chapters, what normally happens is a

Resistance to this emotion, normally expressed through a story in your Chattering Mind about not wanting that experience and emotion to happen. You saw how this Resistance in the Chattering Mind then creates a whole physiological change in your body, reinforcing your Resistance. And this physiological change, in turn, continues to reinforce your Chattering Mind's story making you feel like you are a small, separate self. When you are unaware, you are caught in this unconscious looping, which only exacerbates your strong emotion.

Inquiring into and really *feeling* your feelings and emotions from your Open Mind, instead of unconsciously reacting from your Chattering Mind's story, begins to build the skill of bravely attending to all that you experience. In bravely attending to your experience you are able to respond wisely to your own emotional life. You will see that all feelings are valid and are a natural part of this human life.

Keep It Simple: Bravely Opening to Big Emotions

- When you notice a strong feeling, begin by first dropping your Inner Attention's attachment to your Chattering Mind's story about your emotion.
- Then shift your Inner Attention to the experience of feeling the way the feeling moves through your body.
- Simply practice *feeling* your feelings in your body without getting caught in your story about the feelings.
- Let your Breath Awareness, Body Awareness and Awareness of Silence be anchors for your Inner Attention in the Present Moment.

- When the emotion passes, take note of how your Open Mind and Open Heart are still here. The emotion moved through and you are even more present and grounded because of your courage to open fully.

Note: Sometimes big emotions are just too big to feel alone. It's important when you are feeling overwhelmed by emotion to reach out and seek the support of your parent, teacher, a trusted friend or a counselor.

One of the secrets to any great adventure is to open as fully as you can to what is happening—good, bad or indifferent—and try to respond from your Open Mind and Open Heart instead of reacting from your Chattering Mind. You can even begin to see and relax into the reality of this river of life—thoughts, sensations, experiences and emotions—that is always shifting and changing around you and through your Open Mind and Open Heart. And it is only in this relaxing that you can deeply know, for yourself, who you truly are.

It's as simple, yet as challenging as that, Adventurous One!

CPSIA information can be obtained
at www.ICGtesting.com
Printed in the USA
FSOW03n1441150316
17940FS